THE STORY OF CAPTAIN COOK

THE STORY OF CAPTAIN COOK

by

JOHN LANG

GET ALL OF THE 'HISTORY SHAPERS' BOOKS
The Story of...

David Livingstone	Robert Bruce	Chalmers of New
H. M. Stanley	General Gordon	Guinea
Abraham Lincoln	Lord Clive	Bishop Patteson
Sir Francis Drake	Captain Cook	Joan of Arc
Sir Walter Raleigh	Nelson	Napoleon
Columbus	Lord Roberts	Cromwell

PLEASE NOTE

In this series, you will read about historical figures who displayed courage, bravery, self-sacrifice, and many other admirable traits. Their stories remind us that many people in history took bold actions and made tough choices. Yet, even those who achieved great things sometimes held ideas or pursued goals that were not beneficial to everyone. History is full of complex individuals—parts of their lives inspire us to be brave and stand up for what is right, while other parts remind us to consider the unintended consequences of our actions.

As you explore these biographies, we invite you to reflect on the qualities that enabled these figures to achieve greatness and the lessons we can learn from their mistakes. Maybe you too can become a History Shaper—someone who learns from the past and helps to make our world a better place for everyone.

Contents

Cook's Birth and Boyhood— He Goes to Sea

Towards the close of the year 1728, when George the Second was King of England, there was born in the village of Marton, Yorkshire, a boy whose after life was full of strange adventures and of wonderful discoveries.

This, boy was named James Cook, and he grew up to be one of the most famous men that ever lived. He explored more of the world than any one before him had ever done, and he discovered many islands that are beautiful as fairlyland.

Cook was the son of a Scotch farm labourer who had gone to live and work in Yorkshire. It is not worth calling a journey nowadays, to go from Roxburghshire to Yorkshire, but it was a long, weary way then. There were no railways at that time, nor for many, many, years after, The roads even were so bad that sometimes the coaches could scarcely travel, and at the best they took days to go a distance that now can be covered in a few hours.

Cook's father was very poor. Wages in those days for farm labourers were only a few shillings a week, and he could not afford to go by coach. So he must have walked, over the hills and over the moors, 'till he came to the Cleveland district in Yorkshire, where wages, probably, were much higher than in Scotland.

Here he married, and had a large family, but most of the children died whilst they were very young. James was the second son.

In those days, boys were not troubled much with schools, nor with books. When he was quite a little child; James was set to work on the farm of a Mr. Walker, near Marton. The farmer's wife took an interest in the little boy, and perhaps taught him his letters, but he did not go to any school till later.

When eight years of age, Cook's family moved to Great Ayton, a village about five miles from Marton; where his father, had got work as "hind," or bailiff, to a Mr. Skottowe.

At Great Ayton the boy got what education was possible from the village school—at the best it cannot have been much—and for a time he helped his father in the work of the farm.

When the lad had come to his seventeenth year, he was bound apprentice to a grocer and draper, named Sanderson, in the little fishing village of Staithes.

Where the great cliffs, push out into the ocean, along that part of the Yorkshire coast which stretches north from Flamborough Head, there are 'many deep glens, down which rivulets make their way to the sea. In such a glen lies Staithes, hidden away from the inland world, nestling on the shore of its little bay.

Here James Cook first heard the "call of the sea"—the call that echoes in the hearts of so many boys, and draws them away to be sailors—the call that sets boys wandering all over the world.

Staithes was full of fishermen and of sailors. Of the other people who lived there, some were shipbuilders, and nearly all made their living in some way connected with the sea. What wonder that in a little time Cook wished with all his heart that he had never been bound to a trade! He did not want to be a grocer or a draper. With his whole soul he longed to be a sailor.

Going to sea in those days was a very different thing from going to sea now. There were then no training ships where a boy might partly learn his business, where he might find out if the life of a sailor was likely to be what he had expected, and, if he did not like it, change to something else while there was yet time.

Then, he began at the very beginning, perhaps as ship's boy on a dirty collier, where he was kicked about and rope's-ended by everybody, from skipper to ordinary seaman. His food was bad, and there was not too much of it. He slept where and when he could, and probably got not much of that. He was everybody's servant; everybody might cuff him.

And, some dark winter's night, when a bitter north-east gale was blowing, and the clumsy vessel was beating up against a heavy sea, her decks every few minutes smothered under tons of ice-cold water, if the boy failed to hold on when some wave bigger than common broke on board,—well, what then? "There was no one to blame but himself," probably they might say. No one would trouble very much over it, and in such a sea no boat could be lowered to try to save him. On shore there would be little fuss made. He was only a ship's boy! And his father and his mother would wait long, and would weary, for him who came home never again.

But if a boy lived to grow up, and to become first an "ordinary seaman," and later an "able seaman," even then his life was a poor one.

The food of sailors in those days, even in the King's Navy, was very bad. Salty, terribly salty, beef (called "junk") morning, noon, and night, and not always very much of it. Beef so salty and hard, that even when it was boiled for hours it was as tough as wood, and almost as dry.

The effect of such food, especially if the voyage were a long one, was that sailors fell ill, and many died, of a complaint called scurvy. It was a loathsome disease, and the teeth of men who got it often dropped out. Once it broke out on board ship, nothing could stop it but getting the crew to where they might have fresh vegetables and fresh meat.

The water, too, on board ship was generally bad. It was carried in casks, and the casks were not always very clean, nor were people then very particular about where the water came from. Probably in no long time it had a most evil smell. But the sailors had to drink it; there was nothing else to be got.

For bread they ate biscuit, as hard as stone, and generally full of weevils—a kind of beetle.

The ships were swarming with cockroaches and with rats. Truly a sailor's "lot was not a happy one."

Those, too, were the days of what was called the "press-gang." When in port (and sometimes even when at sea) a merchant sailor always ran the risk of being taken by the press-gang, and forced against his will to serve on board any King's ship that might happen to be short of men.

The press-gang was formed of some of the crew of a ship of the Royal Navy, led by an officer. These men were sent on shore at night to search the public-houses, and all men found there, whether sailors or landsmen, were at once taken prisoners and carried on board the King's ship. Often there were bloody fights before the merchant sailors could be taken; but the man-o'-war's men generally had the best of it. And the law was on their side; the pressed man was wise to make the best of it. The more cheerfully he turned to, and did his work on board, the less likely he was to be flogged.

The "cat o' nine tails" was at work on some ships almost from morning to night. For the smallest fault, perhaps for no fault at all, a brutal captain might order a man to be savagely flogged. "Five dozen" was no great punishment in those bad old days.

But in spite of all, boys ran away to sea. It was in their blood; they could not step on shore.

And James Cook could not stop on shore. Before he had been a year at Staithes he made up his mind that nothing should keep him from being a sailor.

About this time it chanced that he had words with his master. A girl had come into the shop to buy some article, and she had paid for it with a very bright new coin,—what was then called a "South Sea shilling." Cook was so struck by its beauty; that he wanted to have this shilling for himself and he took it, putting into the till in its place a shilling of his own.

But it happened that his master had also noticed this bright coin, and when he found that Cook had got it, he was very angry, almost as angry as if the boy had stolen it.

There was a great dispute. Cook thought that he had done no wrong, because he had put in the till another shilling in place of the new one. His master was so angry that he went to Cook's father about it. The end was that James was taken away from Mr. Sanderson's shop, and apprenticed at Whitby to a Mr. John Walker, a ship-owner. He did not—as has often been supposed—run away to sea. And so began his life as a sailor.

The first vessel in which he sailed was a little collier, named the *Freelove*; the next, the *Three Brothers*, a ship of about 600 tons. On board of the *Three Brothers* he would learn a great deal of his profession, for he helped to rig her, and to fit her out.

From the beginning all went well with James Cook. He was a born seaman.

When his apprenticeship was out, he served as "able seaman" on the *Friendship*, another vessel belonging to Mr. Walker, and of her he soon rose to be mate.

But during all the time of his apprenticeship, and afterwards, whenever he was stopping ashore at Whitby, he constantly read books and studied navigation, never losing a chance of teaching himself anything that might push him on in his profession.

For nine years Cook sailed in these Whitby ships, sometimes going as far as Norway, or to Holland; but for the most part he traded up and down the coast, to and from London.

And then, when he was twenty-seven, there came a change.

Cook Becomes a Man-O'-War's Man

War had broken out between England and France. Cook's ship was then lying in the Thames, and the crew heard that the pressgang was out, taking men from every merchant vessel in port, and sweeping the public-houses and the riverside streets of every man on whom they could lay hands, to complete the crews of the King's ships.

Most of the men hid, for they did not want to serve in the Navy.

Cook too, at first hid himself; for even being mate of a collier might not save him from being "pressed."

But soon he tired of that. It seemed to him it would be much better to enter the Navy as a volunteer.

So he went to Wapping, and as an "A.B." (or able seaman) joined the *Eagle*, a 60-gun ship.

Thus began James Cook's great career in the Navy.

From the first his officers could not fail to see that here was no ordinary man. Even without the help of the letters of recommendation written to Captain Palliser of the *Eagle* by Mr. Walker, Cook's former employer, and by other friends, he would at once have made his mark.

Now began to come in the benefit of his book-reading and studying. And the years that he had passed in the hard life on the Whitby ships in the stormy North Sea were not wasted. For there he had learned every possible point of seamanship. There was nothing on the war-ship, except gunnery, that he needed to be taught. Even as a boy he had been self-reliant, and inclined to hold his own opinion, and, the time during which he had been mate of a collier had added to his confidence in himself. Such a man could not be kept down.

When Cook had been but two years in the Navy, he was made master's mate. With this rank he served on board the *Pembroke*, at the taking of Louisburg, in the Island of Cape Breton. This was when we were fighting the French in Canada in 1758.

The following year he was appointed master of the *Grampus*, but later he was transferred to the *Garland*; and, as it was found that she had already sailed, he was finally appointed to the *Mercury*.

You must understand that the "master" of a ship was not the captain. He was not even a commissioned officer, though the post was not unlike what in the Navy a few years ago was called "navigating lieutenant."

Long ago, three hundred or four hundred years' ago, the captain of a fighting ship was generally a soldier, one who probably knew nothing of sailing, and very little about the sea. He commanded the fighting men, and directed them when the ship was engaged with an enemy. Under him, there had to be a skilled seaman, whose duty it was to sail the vessel from port to port, and to give orders to the, sailors. This man was called the "master," and the, name was still in use in the Navy thirty or forty years ago.

The post of "master" was an important one, and the pay (as pay then went), was better than that of a lieutenant, but a man who became master seldom rose any higher. He had to be a good seaman, skilled in every part of his profession; but generally he was a man without money and without friends to help him on. Often he grew grey in the service, and ended his days without rising higher in rank.

But Cook was not one of those who cease to rise.

On the *Mercury* he sailed for Canada, where his ship joined the fleet which was then helping our troops under the great General Wolfe in the siege of Quebec.

Quebec is a fine city on the river St. Lawrence, and in those days it, and most of Canada, belonged to France.

The entrenched camp of the French troops was at a place near Quebec called Montmorency. To make it possible for our ships to fire into the French camp, soundings of the depth of the river up to that point had to be taken, so that the ships might not get into shallow water and run aground.

To take these soundings was very difficult and very dangerous. Captain Palliser of the *Eagle* advised the Admiral to send Cook on the duty.

It was not possible to carry it out in daylight, because

the French would certainly shoot anybody whom they saw attempting it, so Cook did it all by night. As soon as it was dark enough, he used to start with a few men in one of the ship's boats, with muffled oats, so as to make no noise. Till daylight he would be busy sounding with a lead tied to a line, and noting down in his pocketbook the depths of the different places in the channel, so that he might afterwards draw a chart of the river.

For some nights all went well. But soon the French began to suspect that something was going on, and they set a trap for Cook.

Some tribes of Red Indians, very brave, but very cruel and bloodthirsty men, were fighting against us. The French collected a large number of these men in their birch-bark canoes at that part of the river where they expected Cook and his boat to be in the early morning.

Just at dawn, when the mist was curling up off the water, and the great trees on the banks were beginning to stand out in the dim light like huge black ghosts, the Indians in their canoes stole quietly out and surrounded Cook's boat before he knew that they were near him. Then, with fearful yells, shouting their war-whoops and paddling furiously, they dashed at him.

But Cook never lost his head nor got flurried. There was no possibility of fighting the Indians; they were far too many. So Cook ordered his men to "give way." The boat's crew, bent to their oars, and with straining muscles pulled for dear life. Before the Indians could close on her, the boat slipped through between two of the canoes, and drove hard for the shore. It was a narrow shave. So close to them were the yelling Indians that as Cook and his men tumbled over the bows on to the land, the red men, brandishing their tomahawks and with scalping knives ready, jumped into the stern-sheets of the boat, which they took away with them in triumph. Cook had steered for the shore near to the English Hospital guard, and the Indians did not dare to follow him on the land.

His notes of the soundings of the river were saved, and the chart Cook afterwards drew was so good that it was said that even by daylight the whole thing could not have been better done.

So pleased was the Admiral that after this he employed Cook constantly in making charts of the river below Quebec, where it was dangerous for ships. That work Cook always did splendidly and without mistake.

After this, in 1759, he joined the *Northumberland* man-of-war, and during a winter in Halifax he used all his spare time in reading Euclid, and in studying everything that he thought could help him to get on.

In 1762 he went back to England, and in December of that year he married Miss Elizabeth Batts. But he was not left long at home with his wife. In the following year he was sent out to Newfoundland, where he had already before passed some time; and though he returned to England in the winter, it was only for a stay of a very few months.

In 1764 he was again appointed Marine Surveyor of Newfoundland and Labrador, and he made for the Admiralty charts of all the coast, and explored the country inland where before no white man had ever been.

For several years he was employed in this kind of work, each year adding to the name he was making for himself.

Cook is Raised to the Rank of Lieutenant—He Begins his First Voyage Round the World

In 1768 there came for James Cook another great step upwards. For some years before this date the British Government had been sending out ships to explore the then almost unknown South Seas. The *Dolphin* and the *Tamar*, under Commodore Byron and Captain Mouatt, left England in 1764 and returned in 1766, having sailed round the world, and discovered several islands. Then the *Dolphin*, and the *Swallow*, under Captain Wallis and Captain Carteret, were sent out.

Before these two last-named ships could return, the King decided to send yet another vessel to the South Seas, this time for the purpose of watching what is called the Transit of the bright star Venus across the face of the sun. Astronomers in England knew that this transit would take place in the month of June 1769, and they thought that the best place from which to see it would be one of the islands that had lately been found in those seas.

Now, the Royal Society wanted to send out in this

ship some of their men who knew a great deal about the stars, and they desired that one of these scientific men, a Mr. Dalrymple, should command the ship during the expedition.

But Sir Edward Hawke, who was then at the head of the Admiralty, said that Mr. Dalrymple was not a sailor, and did not belong to the Navy, and that none but a naval man could command a King's ship. Mr. Dalrymple refused to go unless he was made captain.

The Admiralty looked about for the naval officer who would be the best suited to lead such an expedition, and they decided that no one could do better than Mr. James Cook.

Accordingly, in 1768 he was promoted to be lieutenant, and was appointed to the command of the expedition.

So came the second great step in Cook's life.

Not only was he made leader of the expedition, but he was allowed to choose his vessel. He chose a Whitby ship, the *Earl Pembroke*, which was bought by the Admiralty and taken to Deptford to be fitted out. There she was re-christened the *Endeavour*.

Before sailing she was armed with twenty-two guns, and had a crew of eighty-four seamen and marines. When the scientific members of the expedition and their servants came on board, she carried in all ninety-five persons.

She was a Vessel of only 370 tons. A tiny craft she seems to us of the present day, who know better the huge steamships of 10,000 or 12,000 tons. But, small as she might be, she was a giant compared with some of the ships with which Drake sailed two hundred years before, or with those of Cavendish in 1586. Of the three ships commanded by Cavendish, the biggest was of no more than 120 tons; the smallest but of 40 tons. In such cockle-shells men in those days braved the hungry seas and raging weather of that most stormy part of all the world, Cape Horn.

Before the *Endeavour* sailed on her voyage, Captain Wallis, in the *Dolphin*, came home, bringing news of the discovery of Otaheite, one of a group to which Cook afterwards gave the name of the Society Islands. Captain Wallis judged that Otaheite was the spot from which to view the Transit of Venus, and Cook was ordered to make his way to that island.

He left the Thames on 30th July 1768, and dropped down Channel to Plymouth Sound, which he reached in a fortnight. There the *Endeavour* lay waiting for a fair wind till Friday, 26th August, when the real voyage began.

The first place at which the ship called was the beautiful island of Madeira. There, when the anchor was being let go, the master's mate, Mr. Weir, was carried overboard by it, and was drowned. Seamen are very superstitious, and probably most of the crew thought that this mishap had come because their ship had sailed from England on a Friday. That is a day which is believed by sailors to be a very unlucky one.

From Madeira the *Endeavour*, on 18th September,

steered for South America, making for Rio de Janeiro, one of the most beautiful harbours in the world, where she arrived on 13th November.

Fifty-six days is a very long time to take to sail between Madeira and Rio, but ships in those days were very slow.

At first, when starting to sail south from Madeira, there is beautiful weather. Fleecy white clouds float in a sky of sapphire blue, and a wind from the north-east blows steadily. Day follows day, and there is never need to touch a rope nor to trim a sail. Day after day the blue sea sparkles and leaps in the sunlight, crisp, little waves breaking white at the ship's bows. Flying-fish in coveys flash out of the water, and skim away to leeward. The ship bowls steadily along, with a gentle swing that soothes to sleep. At night there is no sound but the lap and swish of the water, and on deck the muffled footfall of the officer of the watch.

But soon this glorious weather ends. When the ship is yet some degrees to the north of the equator, the wind drops. There is a dead calm. The vessel rolls heavily to one side, then, with a sudden jerk, rolls back to the other, every timber and bulkhead creaking and groaning. Hour after hour the useless sails flap with the noise almost of thunder. Now there is no longer any comfort on board. The sun scorches down on the decks till the pitch melts in the seams between the planks; in the cabins the heat is almost too great to let men breathe. A slight puff of wind may come, but before the yards can be braced round and the sails trimmed, it dies away.

Then, maybe, the sky grows inky black; thunder roars with ear-splitting crash, and rain deluges down till the decks swim inches deep.

Some morning, too, very early, over the lonely, heaving, oily-looking sea, perhaps there are seen great waterspouts rearing their heads to the threatening clouds. Around the vessel they stalk, almost as if they were live things that might rush on the ship to overwhelm her.

Ships have lain for weeks in such weather, rolling day and night till their yard-arms almost dip in the sea on either side, never a breeze coming to cheer the hearts of the crew, and to take them out of "the doldrums."

And so it must have been with the *Endeavour*. But at last she drifts into a light air that gives her steerage way. Gradually the breeze freshens from the south-east, till once more she bowls along in fine weather, and Rio is reached.

During the passage from Madeira, the naturalists on board the *Endeavour* discovered new species of sea-birds, and they also found out what causes the sea sometimes to shine and flash during the darkest nights. At times, in the tropics, the appearance is so brilliant that a vessel almost seems to be sailing through an ocean of sparkling jewels. Far astern, the wake left by the ship stretches out like a shining ribbon, and the waves that break against the bows fall back in a foam of fire. Till this voyage, it was not known that this luminous appearance is caused by the presence in the sea of myriads of very small animals, each of which gives out a whitish light.

At Rio, Cook expected to be treated with the same kindness that he had received from the Portuguese at Madeira. But the Brazilian Viceroy was not a very clever man. He could not understand the reason of the *Endeavour* coming to Rio, and he did not believe that sensible people would go so far as Cook said they were going, merely to look at a star. He thought that they must be spies of some kind, and he refused to let anybody from the *Endeavour* go ashore. Even Cook himself was not allowed to land without a Brazilian officer being constantly at his elbow to watch what he did. Cook protested, but it did no good. The Viceroy was too stupid and narrow-minded.

At last, after lying at Rio till 5th December, the *Endeavour* again sailed, after Cook had received a letter from the Viceroy wishing him a good voyage. But she got no farther than the mouth of the bay, for there, Fort Santa Cruz fired into her. The Viceroy had not sent orders that she might leave!

There she was kept for two days, a guard-boat rowing continually round her, till the necessary order came. At last she was allowed to leave her anchorage, and to sail away along the coast on her course to the south. To reach Otaheite (or, as it is now called, Tahiti.), it is necessary to get round Cape Horn, the most southerly point of South America. To get to the west side of this famous cape, there are several ways. One is by the great strait called the Strait of Magellan, which was discovered in 1520 by the Portuguese sailor of that name. Another is by the Strait of Le Maire, much farther to the south, and nearer to Cape Horn. This way was discovered in 1616 by James Le Maire, a Dutch sailor.

It lies between the barren country called Tierra del Fuego and a rocky island to which Le Maire gave the name of Staten. Farther to the south and west are many islands, one of them Horn Island, the south end of which is the dreaded Cape Horn.

Staten, and the other neighbouring islands, lie there lonely and grand, the giant seas eternally dashing themselves in fury against their desolate rocks, and falling back in cataracts of foam on to the clinging seaweed. Almost without cease the wild west wind bellows and roars around their crags. Eternally the great sea-birds wheel and soar over the mountainous waves. Seals and penguins visit their rocks, but other life there is none; all is barrenness and desolation. Plants and trees, where they exist, grow stunted and poor in the shelter of valleys where the foot of man comes never. Out to sea, nothing meets the eye but hurrying-clouds and wild heaving water, white with foam where the monster billows are breaking, pierced now and again by a spouting whale. Truly, "the uttermost end of the earth!"

On 11th January 1769 the Endeavour sighted the coast of Tierra del Fuego. On the 14th she entered the Strait of

Le Maire, a tremendous sea running at the time off Cape San Diego.

Cook anchored several times in the strait, and at the Bay of Good Success, on the mainland, he stayed for a week taking in wood and water.

Here a few of the party, Mr. Banks and Dr. Solander, with some of the crew, went ashore to look for new sorts of plants and animals. On one of their journeys they came near to losing their lives.

They had climbed over a high hill, and forced their way through thick, stunted undergrowth for many hours, till they were quite tired out. Though the season was the middle of summer—January is a summer month south of the equator—the wind was bitterly cold, and a snow-storm came on. Unable to find their way back to the ship, they looked for a sheltered spot where they might light a fire.

But some of the men in the blinding snow had strayed from the rest of the party, and they could not be found. "Whoever sits down will sleep; and whoever sleeps will wake no more," Dr. Solander had told them, when the snow began to fall. Yet the Doctor was the first to sit down to rest, and it was difficult to wake him, and to get him again on his feet. Of the others, three of those who had been separated from the rest of the party were never awakened. In the morning they were found dead. During great cold, when heavy snow is falling, with a high wind, sleep quickly steals over a man who is out in the storm.

"Just a minute I must rest," he thinks; and he sinks down. If he be alone, and no help comes, he wakens no more in this world. Such has been the end of shepherds on the moors, and of other men, even in this country.

Though the cold is so great in the extreme southern parts of South America, the natives wear few clothes. The skin of some animal thrown over their shoulders is almost their only covering; but they smear their bodies with paint, or clay, and their dirt may help to keep them warm. Perhaps, however, in this they are not worse than our forefathers, the ancient Britons.

Whilst the naturalists of the *Endeavour* were using their time in these explorings, Lieutenant Cook was busy taking soundings and bearings everywhere in the strait, so that he might be able to draw correct charts of the coast and islands. He found that the passage by the Strait of Le Maire is very much better and quicker than that by the Strait of Magellan, and much less dangerous.

To get through the Strait of Magellan, Captain Wallis in the Dolphin took three months, and he was many times in great danger, owing to strong currents and often-changing winds. Cook, on the other hand, from opposite the east entrance of the Strait of Magellan round Cape Horn to its western end, was sailing for no more than thirty-three days.

On 26th January 1769 the *Endeavour* left Cape Horn astern, and headed for Otaheite. On the 4th of April she sailed past some of the South Sea Islands, and on the

13th of that month she let go her anchor in Matavai Bay, Otaheite, after a passage of eight and a half months from London.

What a Paradise were these islands to the crew of the *Endeavour* coming direct from bleak and stormy Tierra del Fuego! There, they left snow and bitter weather, barren rocks and cold grey sea; plants and trees few in number, and stunted in growth. Here, they find soft, warm air, and bright sunshine; water sparkling and blue. Birds and butterflies of every gay colour flit amongst the green-leaved bushes, and a gentle breeze whispers through the feathery fronds of the palm trees that grow almost to the edge of the sea.

The natives, too, were very different from those seen in Tierra del Fuego. There they had been dirty, savage-looking, and dull-witted; here they were clean and smiling, their chocolate-coloured skins shining with health. The men were handsome and well-made, and the women, with their pleasant faces, and big, soft brown eyes, seemed like beautiful brown fairies.

None of the natives of Otaheite carried weapons. In their canoes they crowded round the *Endeavour*, and were ever civil and friendly, and ready to help the white men.

But they could not resist stealing whatever they could lay hands on. And this led to trouble.

When Lieutenant Cook, with Mr. Banks and Dr. Solander, and a boat's crew, went ashore to fix on the best spot from which to view the Transit of Venus, they had a small tent rigged in which to rest. To guard this tent, whilst they themselves went farther inland, they left a sentinel and a party of marines, in charge of a midshipman. Scarcely had they got out of sight when one of the natives crept up behind the sentinel, and, snatching away his musket, ran off with it. The midshipman ordered the marines to fire, and the thief was shot dead. Lieutenant Cook was very angry when he heard of this, because he had taken great pains to make friends with the people who lived on the island, and now, through this hasty act, all his trouble was thrown away. Try as he might to reassure them, for some time the natives kept away.

At length they became more confident, and once more sold food and other things to the ship. Beads were chiefly given at first by the crew of the *Endeavour* in exchange for food, but after some days the natives had had enough of the beads, and gave little for them. Then nails were used. For a four-inch nail a native would give as many as twenty cocoa-nuts.

On the 1st of May the observatory from which it was intended to watch the Transit of Venus was finished, and some of the instruments to be used in viewing it were taken ashore and left in a tent, under guard. Next morning, when Lieutenant Cook and Mr. Green went ashore to set up their quadrant (the instrument most necessary for use in observing the transit, and one without which the chief object of the voyage must fail), it was nowhere to be found! The case in which it had been packed was empty.

Search, high and low, failed to find it, and an offered reward was of no effect. The quadrant was gone, though a sentry had never been farther than a few yards from the tent all night.

It was only after long search that the instrument was found by Mr. Banks, hidden away amongst the trees.

On the night of June 2nd, few of the officers of the *Endeavour* slept, so great was their anxiety for a cloud-less day on the morrow, for on the 3rd the transit was to take place.

Luckily there was not a cloud in the sky during the whole of that day, and good sights were got. Thus the first great object of the voyage had succeeded.

But whilst Lieutenant Cook and the others had been busy with their observations, it was found that some of the crew had taken that chance to break into one of the store-rooms. They had stolen a large quantity of nails, in order that they too might do a little trading on their own account with the natives.

This was a very serious theft, because if nails became too common, the natives would cease to value them, and would then give very little food in exchange. All means were tried to find the thieves, but only one of them was caught. He was tied up and given two dozen lashes, but nothing could make him tell the names of the men who had joined him in the theft. Others of the crew, however, were flogged for stealing from the natives, and many were the troubles that came to Cook, either from the thefts of the natives, or from the bad behaviour of his own men.

A short time before the day on which the *Endeavour* was to leave Otaheite, two of the marines one night disappeared. From the natives Cook learned that these men had run away inland, and had married two girls belonging to the island, and that they meant to pass the rest of their lives in Otaheite.

Cook sent a corporal of marines and a petty officer of the ship to try to get the deserters to return to their duty. And as it was of great importance that they should be got, he told some of the native chiefs that till the men returned they themselves would be kept on board ship. The natives on shore, however, when they heard this, sent a message that till the chiefs were set free neither the deserters nor the men sent after them should be returned.

Cook then sent the long-boat with an armed crew, to take them, and to bring them back to the ship. Tootahah, one of the most friendly chiefs, was told that if he wanted to be set free, it would be wise for him to send some of his tribe to help in getting the men back. This had the desired effect. The men were brought in next day, and the chiefs were set at liberty.

When the *Endeavour* sailed from Otaheite on 13th July, two natives, Tupia, who had shown great liking for the English, and a boy of about thirteen, went with the ship, to the great grief of their weeping friends. Tupia was afterwards very useful as an interpreter, and the sight of him on board made the natives of other islands more trustful.

At Huaheine, one of the large islands not far from Otaheite, Oree the king came out in his canoe. As a mark of friendship, he offered to change names with Lieutenant Cook, and until the *Endeavour* sailed he always called Cook "Oree," and himself "Cookee."

Before leaving this group of islands Cook hoisted the Union Jack over, and in name of the King of England took possession of Ulietea, Huaheine, Otaha, and Bora Bora. But they no longer belong to England. Tahiti, and New Caledonia, a magnificent island which Cook discovered on his second voyage round the world, now belong to France. And there are in the Pacific and elsewhere other beautiful islands over which our flag once waved, that have been given up, or have been allowed to slip out of our hands.

Cook Visits New Zealand for the First Time

On 15th August the *Endeavour* sailed towards the south-west, leaving other Islands behind her.

On 6th October, from the masthead a long line of coast was seen, ranges of beautiful hills rising one behind the other; in the far distance vast mountains, white with snow.

"At last," some on board thought, "we have found the Great Unknown Land."

From olden days the belief was general that a huge unknown land lay far to the south. Many had looked for it. In 1642 Tasman, the Dutch sailor, sighted a cape, to which he gave the name of Cape Maria van Diemen, and which he believed was part of that great land.

Now Cook's men imagined that they had found it.

In reality, what they had come upon was the North Island of New Zealand.

A land fair to look upon, a land "flowing with milk and honey," is New Zealand; another England, but with climate finer, and scenery more beautiful. Till Cook landed, no white man since the world began had set foot on its shores. Though Tasman had discovered it more than a hundred years before Cook's day, he feared to land, because on casting anchor, in what he called "Murderers' Bay," he was fiercely attacked by the natives.

The sun does not shine on land more beautiful than New Zealand; a race of people more chivalrous and brave than the Maori does not breathe Heaven's air—nor, it may be said, a race more ready to fight for pure love of fighting.

Long years after the days of Cook, well within the memory of living men, when your fathers were boys, the Maori were fighting against our troops. It chanced that some of our men were surrounded in a "pa" (or fort), and their supply of food, and of powder and shot, was nearly done. The Maori knew the straits that our small force was in, and they knew that a convoy was trying to make its way through the bush to its relief. But they let the convoy with its food and powder come through without attempting to take it.

After the war was over, an officer, who had been shut up in the pa, asked a Maori chief why they had been foolish enough to let such a chance slip through their fingers. It would have been so easy to stop the convoy, and then our men must have surrendered.

The chief stared. "Why," he said, "you fool, if we had taken your powder and your food, how on earth could you have gone on fighting? Of course, we didn't take them!"

On another occasion, when our men tried to storm a pa, an officer and one soldier got in, but the others were beaten back. The officer lay sore wounded and gasping for water. But there was no water in the pa. A Maori chief (who died but a few years ago), climbed over the stockade, ran down the hill under the heavy fire of our men, filled a gourd with water from a stream, ran back again unhurt through the hail of bullets, and gave the water to his wounded enemy. How can one but admire such a people!

It is true that, as Cook discovered, and as the whole world knows, they were cannibals; they ate their enemies whom they slew in battle. But that is a custom which has long since ended.

The day following that on which land had been sighted, the *Endeavour* ran into a bay and dropped anchor at the mouth of a small river. Cook, with Banks and Solander, went ashore in the evening.

There were a few natives standing near where the party landed, and attempts were made to talk with them. But the natives retreated. They would have nothing to say to the strangers. Cook and the others then walked up to some huts near at hand, leaving four boys in charge of the boat. But at once the natives attacked the boat, and one of them was shot dead when about to throw a spear. The others for a moment stood, utterly astonished, and then seizing the dead body, dragged it away with them for some distance. Probably they expected that the white men would eat their slain enemy, if the body were left where it fell.

On the next day three armed boats were sent ashore.

About fifty natives were waiting, seated on the ground. This, Cook's men thought, meant that they were afraid. The party advanced, when at once the natives, tall, strong men, started to their feet and brandished spears, and axes made of greenstone.

Tupia called to them in his own tongue, but these warriors, their fierce faces aflame with defiance, only became the more threatening. A second time Tupia called out. And now they listened and understood. They were willing to trade, Tupia thought, but he warned Cook to beware of treachery.

For the beads and the iron nails that were offered to them they seemed to have no use, but they were willing to give their weapons in exchange for muskets and swords. When this was refused, they became noisy and trouble-some, and one of them suddenly snatched Mr. Green's sword from him, and ran off with it a little way, shouting with joy. The others at once became more threatening, and more and more natives hurried up to join them. Mr. Banks then, at about fifteen yards, fired with small shot at the man who had taken Mr. Green's sword. The man was hit, but even then he did not give up the sword. He retreated very slowly, still waving it over his head. There-upon Mr. Monkhouse fired with ball, and shot him dead.

Far from being frightened, however, the others seemed only the more inclined to attack the white men, and the sword was got back with difficulty. At last a volley of small shot was fired into the crowd, and they then crossed the river and slowly went away.

After this, Cook made a plan to surprise some of the natives and to take them on board ship, so that by kind treatment he might show them that they had nothing to fear, after which he imagined that there would be no further trouble.

Whilst his boats were one day near shore, unable to land owing to the heavy surf that was breaking on the beach, he thought he saw a chance to put his plan in use. Two canoes were seen coming from seaward, one under sail, the other being paddled. Cook ordered his boats to separate, so as to cut off all escape for the canoes. Then they waited. The Maori in the canoe which was being paddled saw the boats, and by hard paddling got away. The other canoe sailed in amongst them before the Maori in her noticed the boats.

Then began a chase. The Maori lowered their sail, and, paddling furiously, were also escaping, when Cook ordered a musket to be fired over their heads. This, he thought, would cause them either to surrender or to jump overboard. But in place of surrendering, the seven men in the canoe at once turned on the nearest boat and fell on the sailors and marines fiercely with stone axes and with their paddles. Such a fight did they make against hopeless odds that at last the marines used their firearms, and four of the Maori were shot dead. The three others, who were but boys, the eldest nineteen and the youngest not more than eleven, at once jumped into the water and tried to swim ashore. With great trouble they were caught and taken into one of the boats.

This unhappy affair was the cause of much sorrow to Lieutenant Cook, and he gave orders that the three boys were to be treated with the greatest kindness on board the *Endeavour*. Two days later they were put on shore, rather against their wish.

Cook thought it wise to leave this part of the coast. No good had come of his visit, and he had been unable to get any supplies for his ship, except of wood. From this fact, he called it Poverty Bay. The south-west point of the bay he named Young Nick's Head, after the boy who first sighted the land.

As the *Endeavour* sailed down the coast southward, many large canoes filled with Maori came off from the land, but seldom could the natives be got to trade. They were too suspicious, and generally they seemed inclined to attack the ship. Muskets fired over their heads had no effect in frightening them, and more than once one of the ship's guns had to be fired, a little wide of them, before they would retire.

Once a Maori was seen wearing over his shoulders the dark-coloured skin of some animal. Cook wanted to get this skin, and in exchange for it offered the man a bit of scarlet cloth. The Maori took off the skin and held it up from his canoe, but would not part with it till he had got the cloth. As soon as that was in his hand, he calmly rolled it and the skin together and paddled off. Neither skin nor cloth was ever got by Cook.

Soon the canoes returned to the ship, this time offering fish. The boy who had come with Tupia from Otaheite was at the time over the side, handing up things which had been bought. Suddenly one of the Maori seized the boy, bundled him into a canoe, which made off. Shots were fired, and some of the men in the canoe were hit. In the confusion Tupia's boy jumped into the sea, and, swimming for his life, was picked up by a boat which the ship lowered to save him.

In remembrance of this attempt by the Maori, Cook named the point of land near at hand Cape Kidnappers. The large bay immediately to the north he called Hawke's Bay, in honour of Sir Edward Hawke. On the shore of this bay now stands the important town of Napier.

The *Endeavour* at this time did not sail much farther to the south, but, when nearly abreast of a bluff which Cook named Cape Turnagain, went about and stood to the north.

All the way up the coast large canoes hurried out from the land, some coming quite close to the ship and looking as if they meant to attack. Everywhere was heard the Maori war-song. Generally, however, they paddled off when one of the ship's guns was fired, though once or twice spears and stones were thrown.

When the ship was abreast of White Island (which is a volcano that still continues to this day to spout flame and smoke), between forty and fifty canoes were seen coming from the land. A few began to trade, but one Maori, seeing some linen hanging over the ship's side, seized it. A musket was fired over his head, but he took no notice. A second musket loaded with small shot was then fired at him. He was hit on the back, but he only gave a shrug of his shoulders and went on packing up the linen. The Maori now dropped astern and began their war-song; but when one of the ship's guns was fired near them, and they saw the ball go skipping over the water, they paddled away in great haste.

At Mercury Bay the *Endeavour* remained a week to get wood and water, and to take sights of the transit of the star Mercury. Here too there was trouble. A Maori made off with some cloth, without giving up what he had agreed to give in exchange, and Lieutenant Gore, seizing a musket, shot him dead. Everywhere, almost, there was the same tale. The Maori "feared no foe."

After rounding Cape Colville, whilst Lieutenant Cook was on shore, many Maori came out, and some went on board the *Endeavour*. A young man stole a small article, and Lieutenant Hicks, who was in command during Cook's absence, ordered him to be seized and flogged. The other Maori ran to the side for their weapons, and those still in the canoes tried to climb on board. But when Tupia told them that the young man was not to be killed, but only flogged, they stood quietly by and watched the punishment. When the flogging was over, the thief's father also gave him a sound beating, and sent him into his canoe.

All along the coast the *Endeavour* sailed, Cook everywhere giving names to the capes and bays and noticeable places.

At the Bay of Islands, when on shore, his party was surrounded by hundreds of natives, who tried to seize the boats. For a time things looked very ugly: it seemed as if there must be a big fight. But Cook's coolness got the party out of the scrape without loss, and the only blood shed was that of a few Maori who were wounded with small shot.

This is the same bay where, two years after Cook's visit, Marion de Fresne, a Frenchman, and sixteen of his crew were killed and eaten by the natives.

As the *Endeavour* began to round the north end of New Zealand, she fell in with storm after storm. From 27th to 31st December it blew without ceasing, a gale, as Cook says in his Journal, "such as I hardly was ever in before," and the sea, he writes, "run prodidgious high." It is always a stormy part of the world, and the ship made little way. Cook says in his Journal, that it is strange that in the summer season she "should be 3 weeks in getting 30 leagues" (30 miles) "to the westward, and 5 weeks in getting 50 leagues" (150 miles).

On 30th December they sighted Cape Maria van Diemen, and thereafter ran down the west side of New Zealand. On 13th January 1770 a "peaked mountain of a prodidgious height," covered with snow, was seen. This Cook named Mount Egmont.

On the 14th they sighted the north end of the South Island of New Zealand. Here, not very far distant from the place in which Tasman had anchored in 1642, in a great bay which Cook named Queen Charlotte Sound, the *Endeavour* remained for some time.

Here also they saw many natives, who again gave trouble. In this place, too, it was clearly proved that the people were cannibals. Parts of a body not wholly eaten were found, and the natives told Tupia that they had a few days before killed and eaten the crew of a canoe which they had taken.

From Queen Charlotte Sound the *Endeavour* sailed through the strait between the North and South Islands, and headed up the east side of the North Island as far as Cape Turnagain, to make quite certain that it was an island. Then, turning, she went round Stewart Island (which Cook supposed was part of the mainland), and so up the west coast to her old station at Queen Charlotte Sound.

Cook sailed past the entrances of the great sounds (or fjords) which have helped to make the scenery of New Zealand famous, and one of them he named Dusky Sound. But he did not venture into any of them, owing to the winds. Nor did he see that highest mountain of all in New Zealand, Mount Cook, which was probably hidden by clouds.

Cook had remained on the coasts of New Zealand

for six months, and the chart which he drew from his observations was a wonderfully correct one. Of it Captain Wharton, RN., writing in 1893, says, "Never has a coast been so well laid down by a first explorer." Cook's work in this respect was always of the best. For some of the islands in the New Hebrides group his charts are used even to this day.

In spite of the many times that the ship was attacked by the Maori, Cook formed a very high opinion of them, and he did not think them a treacherous people, though they were ever ready, indeed anxious, to fight. In his journal, he says that the words the Maori used to shout when they came near the ship meant in English "Come here. Come ashore with us, and we will kill you with our patu patus," (clubs,)—a sort of "Dilly, dilly, come and be killed!"

Let us sincerely hope that the Maori will not, like so many native races, die out through contact with Europeans. But if, unhappily, in the course of time they should do so, it is certain that they will leave in their place a white people who are worthy to rank with them as fighting men. In South Africa the New Zealanders of our own day have shown that they too can fight to the death.

Of the country as a place for white people to settle in, Cook thought very highly, and time has shown how correct was his opinion. There is in the whole world no land more pleasant than New Zealand, none better suited to the British race.

Cook Sails Up the Unknown East Coast of Australia; Thence Home

On 1st April the *Endeavour* quitted New Zealand at Cape Farewell, steering to the west, heading towards that coast which Tasman had named Van Diemen's Land, and which was then thought to be a part of New Holland (Australia).

A heavy gale drove Cook farther to the north than he had meant to go. On Thursday the 19th of April 1770 land was sighted, and named Point Hicks, after Lieutenant Hicks, who was the first to see it. This is on the coast of what is now the Colony of Victoria, S.W. from Cape Howe; but the country was then called by Cook New Wales, and later, New South Wales. As the *Endeavour* sailed up the coast, Cook gave to various places the names that are now so well known—Cape Howe, Mount Dromedary, Point Upright, the Pigeon House, and others. The country he describes as of "a very agreeable and promising aspect," and from the numbers of fires that were seen he judged that it was inhabited.

At one point, the ship having run very close inshore, he

tried to land where several natives were seen, with canoes drawn up on the beach, but the surf was too heavy. This was near what is now known as Bulli.

At daylight next morning a bay was discovered which seemed to be well sheltered from all winds. Into this the *Endeavour* was taken, and her anchor let go about two miles inside the entrance. On both sides as they sailed in, natives were seen, men, women, and children. But these all disappeared when Cook, with Banks and Solander, and Tupia, and a boat's crew, made towards the shore. A few of the men came back, brandishing Spears, and one of them threw a stone at the boat. Cook fired a musket, but the man took no notice, and when Cook fired again with small shot and hit one of them, it only had the effect of making him snatch up a shield. Cook and the others then landed, when a few spears were thrown by the natives without hitting any one, and the men slowly went away. As Mr. Banks was afraid that the spears which were thrown might be poisoned, they were not followed up.

Tupia had tried to get them to talk, but nothing they said could be understood. Close by were some huts made of bark, in one of which there were four or five children, to whom beads and other things were given. But these presents were all found next morning untouched in the empty huts, and as long as the ship remained, by no means could the black-fellows be got to make friends.

Probably there had been heavy autumn rains some time before Cook arrived in the country, for he speaks of "good grass" and "fine meadow" everywhere, and no doubt the soil was ablaze with wild-flowers. He adds that "the great quantity of plants Mr. Banks and Dr. Solander found in this place occasioned my giving it the name of Botany Bay." But he probably gave it this name some time later, for at first it was called Stingray Bay from the numbers of stingrays the sailors caught there, and by this name it was known in the Admiralty chart.

On the 6th of May, after leaving Botany Bay, the ship was "abreast of a bay wherein there appeared to be safe anchorage, which I called Port Jackson" (after Mr.— afterwards Sir George—Jackson, one of the Secretaries of the Admiralty).

Had Cook but gone inside the Heads of Port Jackson, he would have found "safe anchorage" for all the fleets of the world in that most splendid of harbours, on whose shores now stands the great city of Sydney. But it was not till eight years later that the wonders of Port Jackson became known, when Captain Philip explored it in his boats from Botany Bay, that place of ill omen to so many persons on his fleet of convict ships.

Thereafter, as the *Endeavour* went north, Cook named many places now well known—Broken Bay, Port Stephens, Cape Hawke, Smoky Cape, Point Danger, and very many others. Everywhere he mentions seeing smoke on shore, and signs of inhabitants.

And now, having passed Moreton Bay, Harvey Bay, and Cape Capricorn, as she drew farther and farther to the north, the ship began to get into waters the navigation of which even at this day is of great danger, owing to the vast number of reefs and shoals scattered everywhere in the sea: What must it have been in Cook's day, when no charts existed, and he had to feel his way up the coast! It is very wonderful that he did not leave the bones of the *Endeavour* somewhere on the Great Barrier Reef. And, indeed, one fine moonlight night it came very near doing so.

The ship was under easy sail, and soundings were constantly being taken of the depth of the water. The man at the lead had just sounded and found 17 fathoms (that is 102 feet in depth). Before he could again heave the lead the ship struck, and stuck fast. She had struck the edge of a reef of coral rocks. In some places around her the water was 24 feet deep; in others, not more than 3 or 4 feet. There the *Endeavour* remained for twenty-four hours. Luckily the weather was fine.

Her guns and many other things were thrown overboard to lighten her, and at last with great difficulty she was got off. But even then it seemed likely that she would sink, so much water was leaking into her. And if she sank, how were Cook and his men ever to get home? There was no one to help them, no one much nearer than 2000 miles.

Soon after the ship was got off the rocks, and before they could find any bay or harbour in which they could repair her, it began to blow. For three days this dirty weather continued, whilst the *Endeavour* lay at anchor a mile from the shore, and all this time the crew had to keep pumping out of her the water that continually leaked in.

When the weather grew finer, the anchor was got up, and the ship ran for a harbour that had been found, but on the way in she twice ran ashore. The second time, she stuck fast, and was not got off till the next day.

Everything was now taken out of the ship, and she was hauled into very shallow water, where the tide left her almost dry, and the leak was got at and repaired. The coral rocks had cut clean through several of her planks, and a big bit of rock still stuck in one of the holes.

Whilst this work was going on, parties were often sent inland to try to get provisions, but very little could be found. Curious-looking animals were seen, and some were afterwards shot, which Mr. Banks learned from the natives were called kangaroos. This was the first time that kangaroos had ever been seen by white men.

On 6th July the repairs to the ship were finished, as far as it was possible to do them. She was refloated, and her water, and stores, and remaining guns were got on board during the next few days.

Where the *Endeavour* was beached the town of Cooktown now stands. Twenty years ago the people of that town tried, without any success, to recover from the sea the brass guns that were thrown over-board when the ship was on the reef.

On the 9th the master, who had been out to sea in a boat trying to find a channel for the *Endeavour* to sail through, came back bringing three turtles weighing 791 lbs., and all hands had a feast. Except fish, the crew had now been without fresh meat for four months, so this must have been a great treat to them.

On the 18th and 19th several natives came on board and appeared to be very friendly; but they wanted to take ashore with them two turtles which had been caught, and which were on the deck. When this was refused, they became sulky and troublesome, and soon left the ship. Afterwards, when Cook was on shore, one of them took a handful of dry grass, and lighting it at a fire, ran round the party in a wide circle, everywhere setting a light to the grass. This started a great bush fires which went raging away amongst the trees and some of the ship's stores were burned. Luckily, very little had been left ashore. The natives also did the same thing round the place where the ship's nets and linen were spread out to dry, and Cook was obliged to fire at them with small shot before they would stop trying to burn him out.

It was not until the 4th August that the *Endeavour* got away from this spot, and as she kept groping her way up the coast, many times she was in the greatest danger.

At last, on 16th August, there came a time when it did not seem possible to save her. During the night the wind fell to a dead calm, and though no bottom could be found when sounding even at a depth of more than 800 feet, the roaring of surf could be plainly heard at no great distance. At dawn, great, foaming breakers were seen not a mile from the ship, and she was drifting down fast into them. There was no possibility of anchoring in water so deep, and though the boats were got out and the ship's head pulled round away from the breakers, she still continued to drift down, and soon she was less than a hundred yards from them. In his journal, Cook writes, "The same sea that washed the side of the ship rose in a breaker prodidgiously high the very next time it did rise, so that between us and destruction was only a dismal valley the breadth of one wave, and even now no ground could be felt with 120 fathom" (720 feet).

No one who has not seen a coral reef, and the sea breaking over it, can know how grand and terrible is the sight, how awful the roar and thunder of the furiously breaking sea. Nothing that gets into it can live, and the vessel that is flung on such a reef is smashed to matchwood in less than a minute.

When the *Endeavour* had drifted so near that to everybody it seemed that they had but a few minutes to live, a light air was felt, hardly enough to fill the sails. The men in the boats towing her pulled for their lives, and slowly she widened her distance from the breakers. For the moment she was saved.

But again the same fearful time had to be gone through. Again the wind died away, and once more she drifted towards the hungry breakers. At last, but not until the next day, a steady breeze sprang up, and she slipped through a narrow opening in the reef, and anchored in quiet water.

From now onwards Cook had a boat going constantly ahead of the *Endeavour*, looking out for shallow water. In this way he slowly rounded the most northerly point of Australia, which he named Cape York, and felt his way along *Endeavour* Strait, between what is now known as Thursday Island and the mainland.

By this voyage Cook proved that New Guinea did not form part of New Holland, (an error into which all the maps of that time fell;) but he thought that probably islands or reefs extended all the way from *Endeavour* Strait to New Guinea, which is not far from the truth.

It is curious to read in Cook's Journal his opinion of New Holland—or Australia, as we now call it. Though he saw but a fringe of the coast, and landed seldom, it shows how correct was his judgment to find him saying, "... It can never be doubted but that most sorts of grains, fruits, roots, etc., of every kind would flourish here were they once brought hither... and here are provender for more cattle at every season of the year than can ever be brought into the country."

On 25th August the *Endeavour* quitted the Australian coast, heading for New Guinea, which she sighted on the 29th, after at least one very narrow escape from total loss on a reef. Everywhere along this part of the coast the water was very shallow, and it was not until 3rd September that Cook landed. Many natives were seen, all hostile, and Cook did not think it worth while to waste time in New Guinea. Provisions were now very short, and he wanted to get to Batavia, in Java, where he expected to get supplies from the Dutch.

On the way to that port, the *Endeavour* sighted the little known island of Savu. Here he landed, and after much haggling with the Dutch Governor he bought seven buffaloes and many fowls, a supply of food of which his crew stood in great need.

On 10th October the ship anchored at Batavia, without one single man on the sick list, a record for those days most extraordinary. "Lieutenant Hicks, Mr. Green, and Tupia," Cook says in his Journal, "were the only people who had any complaint occasioned by a long continuance at sea." Never before had a vessel been known to come through a long voyage without many of the crew dying of scurvy. And to Cook's constant care of his men, of their, and of the ship's, cleanliness, and of their food, this was due.

But at Batavia his luck in that respect deserted him.

The ship remained at that port, being repaired, until 26th December, on which date she sailed for the Cape of Good Hope with upwards of forty sick on board. The rest of the crew also were in a feeble state, all having been down with fever, except the sailmaker, an old man of over seventy, who, Cook says, "was more or less drunk every day."

In all, during the voyage, the *Endeavour* lost, from all causes, thirty-eight men out of her total of ninety-five. Of these, thirty died at, or after leaving, Batavia. On 24th

January 1771, at sea, Corporal Trusslove died; on 25th, Mr. Sporing; 27th, Mr. Parkinson and Ravenhill, the old sailmaker; on 29th, Mr. Green; 30th, Moody and Hake, two of the crew; and on the 31st four more of the crew died. And so it went on. Tupia and his boy had died at Batavia, and later, Lieutenant Hicks died at sea.

The Cape of Good Hope was reached on 14th March, and here she remained till 15th April, when she sailed for England.

On Saturday, 13th July 1771, the *Endeavour* once more dropped anchor in the Downs.

Cook is Promoted, and Starts on His Second Voyage

The voyage of the *Endeavour* was the greatest and the most successful that had ever been carried out. No honour is too great for the man whose energy and perseverance made it possible. In his "Life of Captain Cook," Sir Walter Besant has well said: "He had given to his country Australia and New Zealand—nothing less: he had given to Great Britain, Greater Britain."

Great was the excitement in England over this voyage. The King sent for Cook, and everywhere the people did honour to the brave sailor. From a collier's boy he had risen to be the most-talked-of man in England. And now he was "Captain" Cook, for the Admiralty had promoted him to the rank of commander.

But of all the people who made much of him, there was none more glad to see him than Mary Prowd, Mr. Walker's house-keeper at Whitby. This old lady had been kind to James Cook when he was an apprentice boy, and later, when he was mate of a coal ship, and her pride in him had never failed. Now she was wild with joy when she heard that he was coming to visit Whitby.

But people told her that things were very different now, and that she must not call him "James." She must remember his rank, and what a great man he was. She was told she must call him "Captain." All of which Mary promised to remember. And so she did, till the great Captain Cook came into her room. Then away to the winds went all she had been taught. "Eh! honey James, how glad a's to see thee," she sobbed, and clasped him in her arms.

Captain Cook's stay in England was not a long one. Much as he may have wanted rest and a long stay at home, (where, during his absence, two of his children had died), there was little chance of rest for him.

He was in England just one year, many months of which were taken up by hard work, either connected with his last, or in getting ready for his next voyage round the world.

The idea of the Great Unknown Land still filled men's thoughts, and it was said that Cook's last voyage had not proved that there was no such land, but only that it was not in the part of the world that he had visited. He was now ordered to go in search of that Unknown Land, farther to the south than he had sailed in the *Endeavour*.

Bouvet, a French sailor, had said that in 54° south latitude, he had seen a part of this land, and Cook was told to make his way there, and if in the latitude and longitude named by Bouvet he could not find land, then he must go on still farther to the south. Men said that there were Europe and Asia and most of America on the north side of the equator, there must also be a huge unknown land on its south side; otherwise, they thought, the world would not keep its balance. And in this Great Unknown Land, when it should at last be discovered, what vast treasures of gold, and of silver, and of precious stones, might they not expect to find!

On 13th July 1772, Cook sailed in the *Resolution*, a vessel of 462 tons, and having with him a smaller ship, the *Adventure*, of 336 tons, commanded by Captain Tobias Furneaux. Both were Whitby ships, built on the same lines as the *Endeavour*. With Captain Cook sailed several of the officers and men who had been with him in his first voyage round the world.

Touching at Madeira and the Cape of Good Hope, the *Resolution* and *Adventure*, from the last-named port, pushed on south into the stormy Southern Ocean.

Now all day there is the humming of wind in the rigging, and the vessels stagger and plunge in the tumbling grey sea. Albatrosses, petrels, and hosts of sea-birds wheel around the ships, or follow in their wake, looking for food. As the hours and days go by, the noise of the wind comes louder and wilder, till men's voices can scarcely be heard through its wailing. From out of the mist, great seas, like mountains with deep valleys between, rush down on the ships, toss them towards the heavens, and roar away to leeward. Tons of water thunder down on the decks, bursting through the skylight and flooding the cabins.

To those sitting down below by the smoking lamp, when the darkness has fallen, it is a time of trouble, a time not without fear. From the deck they hear a hoarse voice bellow, "Stand by your fore-topsail halyard," followed by the rush of men's feet. A wild yell:—then a hubbub as of Bedlam; a loose sail beating in the wind with the noise of thunder, blocks thumping, wind howling, and sea roaring. And the squall heels the ship over and still over, till it seems almost easier to walk on the bulkheads at the side of the cabin than on the sloping deck.

The weather grows bitter cold, and out from the mist around the ship come the strange sighing noise of a blowing whale, and the melancholy cry of penguins. Sudden squalls of snow whiten the decks and the rigging, and blind the lookout man. From a bank of fog and swirling snow glides a ghostly, flat-topped, blue-grey shadow, against whose sides the sea breaks in fury, sending the flying spray shooting hundreds of feet into the air. An iceberg! And all round are huge cakes of floating ice, which crash against the sides of the ship.

From early in December till the middle of March Captain Cook pushed on through the ice and bitter weather, looking for land, but finding none. Though it was the middle of the Antarctic summer, the rigging and tails of the *Resolution* were often covered with ice, and the men suffered from the cold and the constant dampness of everything on board. Scurvy broke out, though no one died of it. Every case was treated as Captain Cook directed, and all recovered.

On 8th February 1773, in a thick fog, the *Adventure*

parted company with the *Resolution*, and was not again seen. Till the end of her voyage in these seas the *Resolution* was now alone.

On 16th March, the summer season being now near an end, the ship was headed for New Zealand, where Cook hoped to find the *Adventure* waiting for him. On 26th March she anchored in Dusky Bay, one of the sounds on the west coast of the South Island of New Zealand, which he had named on his first visit to that country. Here she lay for more than a month, snugly moored in deep water, so close to the land that the men could go ashore by a tree which overhung the deck.

How beautiful the green leaves and the ferns and the flowering plants and shrubs must have looked to those men, fresh from the ice of the Antarctic; how quiet and peaceful the life, to those who for so long had seen little but fog and bad weather and mountainous seas.

The *Resolution* had arrived in Dusky Sound with only one sick man on board; but Cook was not satisfied to let well alone is that respect. He made a kind of spruce beer from some of the trees and shrubs, which was said to be "very refreshing and medicinal," and it was served out to the crew daily. He was always sending boats ashore to collect all kinds of plants—scurvy-grass, wild celery, and others—which he thought might be useful in preventing scurvy, and these plants were boiled with the men's food. In this way he kept the ship almost clear of that dreaded disease, and he did not lose one single man from scurvy during the whole voyage. Very different was the case of the *Adventure*, amongst whose crew the disease broke out over and over again, and carried off several of the men. Captain Furneaux was not so careful as Captain Cook in making his men eat the wild vegetables when they could be got.

But if the men on the *Resolution* were in good health, the sheep and the goats on board were not. These poor beasts, as well as a great many pigs, had been brought by Cook for the purpose of being put ashore in New Zealand and other places, in the hope that they might increase and in time spread all over the islands. But the cold and wet and the want of fresh food during the voyage in the Antarctic seas had killed many, and those that still lived were ill of scurvy. When put ashore at Dusky Sound the poor brutes could not eat, their teeth had become so loose. Whilst the *Resolution* lay in Dusky Sound, a few natives were seen, all of whom were very friendly, but they disappeared before the vessel sailed. On 29th April she left the sound by a new channel, but this was so winding and difficult that it was not until 11th May that she reached the open sea.

At Queen Charlotte Sound the *Adventure* was found lying at anchor after losing the *Resolution* in the fog she had cruised near the spot for some days, when, still seeing no signs of her, she had steered to the east, but in a latitude much farther to the north than the track of the *Resolution*. Afterwards she headed for Van Diemen's Land, part of the coast of which she explored, without seeing any natives. The *Adventure* discovered some islands to the east of Van Diemen's Land, which were named Furneaux Islands, and she sighted the coast of Australia, but when she came away from that coast, Captain Furneaux still believed that Van Diemen's Land was part of New Holland.

Leaving Queen Charlotte Sound, the two vessels sailed to the south-east till 27th July without falling in with any land, and then they headed to the north for Otaheite, sighting on the way many islands. But at Otaheite the end of their voyage had nearly come. On 16th August, as the ships crept slowly in towards the reef, the wind failed them, and they lay rolling helplessly in the heavy swell. The boats could not tow them off, and quickly the ships drifted nearer and nearer to destruction. As a last chance, the *Resolution's* anchor was let go. But the water was too deep; still she drifted closer to the thundering breakers. At last, in three fathoms water (18 feet) the anchor held. But it was too late, Already she was in the foam of the breaking rollers, and as each sea left her she bumped heavily on the coral reef. The *Adventure*, being smaller, was held by her anchor before she touched ground.

It was now the hour for the sea breeze to spring up, as at that season it does daily in this part of the world. If it had blown that day as usual, nothing could have saved the two vessels; they must have been dashed to pieces on the reef. But the hours went by, and still the dead calm continued. At last the tide turned; a light breeze off the land began to blow, slowly growing stronger, till both ships were able to raise their anchors and sail into safety.

At Otaheite the natives were again friendly, and many were the inquiries for Tupia. Many, too, were the thefts, as on the visit of the *Endeavour*. One chief this time went so far as to gather together the empty cocoa-nuts which had been thrown overboard from the ships after the milk had been taken out of them. These he then tied in bundles, as if they were fresh, and sold them over again to the men.

At Huaheine also (where King Oree still called himself "Cookee"), there was the same thieving. Once, when Dr. Sparrmann, a Swedish naturalist who had joined the *Resolution* at the Cape of Good Hope, went ashore by himself to collect plants, he was set upon by two men, who stripped him, took away all his clothes, and then beat him with the flat of his own sword.

On 7th September the two ships sailed, the *Adventure* taking with her a man whose name was Omai, a native of Ulietea, and on the *Resolution* went a native of Bora Bora, named Oedidee.

On 23rd September, about a week after leaving Ulietea, Hervey's Island was discovered, a beautiful island covered with cocoa-nut palms, but, so far as could be seen from the ships, without any people. The vessels then sailed through the Friendly Islands group, which Tasman had discovered in 1643. At Middleburg, one of the islands, Cook was the only man bold enough to taste a bowl of "kava," which was offered by a chief. And indeed it is no great wonder that the others did not care to take any. As Dr. Young says in his "Life of Captain Cook," it "was brewed, as in other South Sea Islands, by the natives chewing the root; spitting out the juice into a bowl, and then diluting it with water." It does not sound very nice—even though the water happened to be the water (or milk) from the inside of a cocoa-nut. At Tongataboo, another island of the same group, more "ava" was offered, but one does not know that Cook's courage was equal to a second dose.

Cook in the Antarctic Ice—His Discovery of New Caledonia—Massacre of the Adventure's Boat's Crew in New Zealand.

From Tongataboo the *Resolution* and *Adventure* sailed back to New Zealand. Off Cape Kidnappers canoes came out, and Cook gave the natives potatoes, and seeds of turnips, parsnips, and other vegetables, as well as pigs and fowls. Wherever he went he sowed seeds, and turned loose fowls, pigs, and goats, and sometimes sheep. The sheep died, or were killed, but the wild pigs of New Zealand at this day are the descendants of those turned loose by Cook.

Very stormy weather, with now and again days without a breath of wind, prevented the ships from getting through Cook's Strait to Queen Charlotte Sound. Several times they were blown out to sea, and at last, after having twice parted company with the *Resolution*, the *Adventure* disappeared altogether, and never rejoined her. Captain Furneaux had been told that if the ships should be parted by bad weather, they were each to make for Queen Charlotte Sound. But when the *Resolution* anchored there on 3rd November there was no sign of the *Adventure*. Cook waited till 25th, November. On that day he sailed, having first buried under a tree, on which was carved "Look beneath," a bottle with a message enclosed for Captain Furneaux telling him where to follow the *Resolution*. Whilst the ship was in Queen Charlotte Sound, Cook and his officers, to their great horror, actually saw the Maori eat part of a young man whom they had killed.

The *Resolution* now once more steered for the Antarctic, and on 12th December, in latitude 62° 10' the first iceberg was seen. From now onwards they were amongst ice and fog and snow, and Christmas Day was spent in bitter weather, nearly a hundred icebergs being round the ship. Still Cook pushed on, looking for that great continent which he now began to think did not exist.

At length, in latitude 71° 10', a higher south latitude than any one before him had ever reached, he came on ice so close packed and dense that it was not possible to sail any farther. As far as the eye could reach on either side as they skirted along the edge, there was nothing to be seen but ice; no open water anywhere, nothing but vast fields and mountains of ice.

For the time, Cook gave up the attempt to find land in this Antarctic region, and the ship was again headed to the north, where in latitude 38° Cook meant to look for land said to have been found in olden days by Juan

Fernandez. But nothing of this land could be seen, and the *Resolution* was now headed for Easter Island.

Before reaching this land, Cook, who had been ailing for some time, fell so ill that he could not leave his bed. For more than a week he was in violent pain, and at one time it was thought that he must die.

Sick people, when they begin to get well from a severe illness, sometimes take strange fancies, and the fancy that seized on Captain Cook was a very strange one. There was no fresh meat on board, and though at other times he could eat anything, however rough and tasteless, now he craved for something more inviting than salt junk. There was on the *Resolution* a dog belonging to Mr. Forster (one of the naturalists of the expedition), and Cook's fancy was that he could eat a little fresh meat, even a bit of dog. The poor animal was therefore killed and made into broth, which Cook ate and greatly enjoyed. After this he quickly got well. The Chinese eat dogs, and the Maori did so in Cook's day, but white men have not often killed one for food, except when terribly pressed by hunger, when nothing else could be got.

On 11th March 1774 Easter Island was sighted, and two days later the *Resolution* anchored near a smooth, sandy beach. Here the natives were friendly, but, as usual, stole everything they could lay hands on.

On this island were found huge stone figures of men, some of them that had fallen down measuring from 15 to 27 feet, but others that were still standing seemed to be even higher. A few of these statues are now in the British Museum.

There being no wood nor water for the ship on Easter Island, Cook sailed for the Marquesas, where a new island was discovered. Here again it was the old story of thieving by the natives, and one man was shot dead whilst trying to take away in his canoe an iron stanchion belonging to the ship.

After this it was difficult to get any of the natives to trade, but when at last they again began to bring food for sale, the market was spoiled by one of the officers foolishly giving in exchange for a pig a large quantity of bright red feathers which he had got at Tongataboo. The natives were so pleased with the feathers that they would not sell for any thing else, and beads and nails became of no value. As there were no more feathers on board, no more food was to be got.

From the Marquesas the *Resolution* headed again for Otaheite, passing on the way many small islands, which made the sailing very dangerous. Many of these islands were so low-lying that if it had not been for the protecting coral reef the big waves must have washed clear over. All were covered with palm trees, and all were very beautiful. A few were round in shape, and in their centre lay a quiet lagoon or lake of water so still and clear that even at great depths the bright-coloured fishes could be seen swimming amongst the coral branches.

At Otaheite, Huaheine, and Ulietea, islands where

most of the crew would willingly have passed the rest of their lives in sleepy idleness, the *Resolution* remained in all about six weeks, when she sailed to the west, leaving Oedidee at the last-named island. Oedidee was in great grief at being left behind, but Captain Cook did not care to take him farther.

Palmerston Island and Savage Island were now discovered. On landing at Savage Island, Cook and his party were at once attacked by the natives, and Dr. Sparrmann was hit by a stone thrown at him. Muskets were fired, and the natives fled; but it was thought wise for the party to get on board the boats again.

A second landing was made farther along the coast, and here again the natives attacked as viciously as wasps when their nest is touched. One spear that was thrown passed just over Captain Cook's shoulder, whereupon he tried to shoot the man who threw it, but his musket missed fire. After some fighting the natives again fled, but Cook made no other attempts to land on this island.

Many small islands were passed after this, and some of the larger were visited. Then, on 16th July, land discovered by Quiros in 1606 was sighted, and some days later the islands of Ambrym and Mallicollo (part of the New Hebrides group) were discovered. In some of these islands the natives to this day are cannibals. It is not more than ten years since the natives of Ambrym took a young Englishman who was trading in the island and shut him up in a kind of cage. There they kept him for some weeks, feeding him on the best of everything and treating him with the greatest kindness. But kindness was not their motive in so feeding him. Daily they used to inspect him and playfully pinch him, till, judging that he was now fat enough, they killed and ate him.

Amongst these wild people, in spite of the fact that they were armed with bone-pointed arrows, the heads of which were covered with a dark sticky substance which was thought to be poison, Captain Cook went many times alone, and with nothing in his hand but the green branch of a tree. Each time he was well received, and no attack was made on him; but he ran great risk, for the New Hebrideans are very fierce and warlike. These were, however, the only islands visited by the *Resolution* where nothing was stolen by the natives.

The people of the New Hebrides are an ugly race, not like those of Tahiti and of other islands in the Pacific. Their skins are not of the beautiful, rich chocolate colour that is found on many South Sea Islands, but are so dark as to be almost black. The men are much shorter than the Tahitians, being seldom more than 5 feet 4 inches in height, and their limbs are poorly developed. Their heads are small and not well shaped; the foreheads are low and receding, and the skull in many cases slopes on either side to a ridge, almost like the roof of a house.

At the islands of Erromanga and Tanna, farther to the south-east, the *Resolution's* crew had more fighting. At Erromanga four savages were shot, and two of the sailors were wounded with arrows. At Tanna, a volcano, about four miles to the west of the ship's anchorage, gave much trouble: Almost without ceasing it continued to belch out fire and smoke, and the ashes which it threw out covered the ship with a fine dust which got into everybody's eyes, and made its way into the food and everywhere on board. Often, with terrific roaring, it threw up stones to a tremendous height. When rain fell, the dust from the volcano came down in the shape of mud.

Back from Tanna the ship went to the coasts of Mallicollo and Espiritu Santo, and thence heading to the south-west she discovered, after four days' sail, one of the largest islands in the South Pacific, which Cook named New Caledonia. A beautiful island is this, full of minerals of all kinds, with a fine climate, and in the lower-lying parts capable of growing almost anything. Within the reef which protects it from the giant rollers of the Pacific are fine harbours, such as that of Nouméa, where fleets might lie in safety.

And this magnificent island, 270 miles long, might have been ours! But since 1863 it has belonged to France. Truly it is a land where "only man is vile." The sole use to which the French Government has put it is that of a great convict station, where thousands of men and women, the scum of French prisons, are kept, guarded by thousands of soldiers. Little work, has been done in the island, and there are few roads, and no railways. The place is a "dumping" ground for criminals. Indeed, it is very vile, and the vileness, overflowing, sometimes escapes to our own Australian Colonies, there to be a thorn in the flesh of our kith and kin.

The most beautiful part of New Caledonia, the Isle of Pines, is now used solely as a prison for men under "life" sentences. When the *Resolution* sighted this island the land was seen to be covered with what seemed to be long straight columns, which at first were thought to be basaltic, like the Giant's Causeway in Ireland. On reaching the shore, however, it was found that these were pine trees. Hence the island was called the Isle of Pines. The pine of New Caledonia grows to a great height, but has very short, straight branches. From a distance the trees look most strange, and like nothing so much as gigantic hairy asparagus.

The navigation near the south end of New Caledonia is very dangerous, owing to the many rocks and shoals, and the *Resolution* more than once ran great risk of going ashore. Getting out of this dangerous spot, the ship was headed again for Queen Charlotte Sound, which she reached on 18th October, after having discovered on the voyage Norfolk Island. This lovely island was then quite uninhabited. It was afterwards used by us for a time as a place to which convicts were sent from Botany Bay, and thus, what was once a peaceful Paradise, became a spot more full of misery and horror than words can tell.

The *Resolution* remained about a month in New Zealand, laying in stores of salted fish and other things for use in their next attempt to find the Great Unknown Land, which Cook this time meant to look for to the south of Cape Horn.

Whilst she lay in Queen Charlotte Sound; it could plainly be seen that the natives had something on their minds, but what this was could not be found out. Some of them talked of having killed white men, but others denied that anything of the kind had taken place. It was not till long afterwards that Cook got a full account of the terrible thing that had happened.

The *Adventure*, he learned, had come into Queen Charlotte Sound a few days after he had buried his message for Captain Furneaux. She had there remained some time, and a day before sailing had sent a boat's crew under two midshipmen, Mr. Rowe and Mr. Woodhouse, to gather wild celery. The boat was ordered to return to the ship the same evening, but she never came back.

Another boat, under Lieutenant Burney, was sent next morning to look for the missing men. After a long search, Burney came on six large canoes, and near them saw great numbers of Maori. Farther along the shore were more natives, but from none of them could he get any word of the missing boat. At last, some shoes were found, one of which was known to have belonged to Mr. Woodhouse. Then a white man's hand, tattooed "T.H." in the same way that the hand of Thomas Hill, one of the missing men, had been tattooed. Then a broken oar, sticking upright in the sand. Lastly, an awful sight, that made men sick with horror!

The heads and hearts and lungs of the boat's crew lay around, and dogs gnawed parts of the bodies that had not already been eaten by the Maori. Nothing was seen of any of the men alive.

Some of their clothes and a few shoes were got, and the hand of Thomas Hill, a hand known to be Mr. Rowe's, and the head of Captain Furneaux's black servant, were taken aboard the *Adventure*, and afterwards buried. The natives all disappeared, and the ship had therefore no chance of punishing them. The *Adventure* then sailed towards Cape Horn, and on the way she passed the spot where Bouvet had said that land existed, but without seeing any signs of a coast-line. From this she headed for the Cape of Good Hope, and thence to England, which she reached nearly a year before Cook's return.

The *Resolution* left New Zealand on 10th November, and made a good passage the west side of the Strait of Magellan. Thence Captain Cook set out to explore the stormy ocean to the south of Cape Horn.

In many charts of that day land was laid down in this part of the Southern Ocean, and it was believed to exist. In no case, however, did Cook find those charts to be correct, and the *Resolution* sailed over the spots where in the charts land was marked. But on 14th January 1775 a large island was seen, which Cook named South Georgia. On this desolate spot he landed. Mountains and valleys alike were covered with deep snow, though this was the height of the summer season, and all along the coast were great cliffs of ice. No trees or plants were seen, nor anything growing but grass in tufts, and, where the snow was swept from the ground by the wind, moss. Except seals and sea-birds, no living thing was to be seen.

Through storm and fog the *Resolution* pushed on south, till, in latitude 60°, mid iceberg and much floating ice, land was again seen. This Cook named Sandwich Land. Still farther to the south were more islands, but as he now thought that his discoveries had clearly shown that no Great Unknown Land existed in the far south, and as the rigging and sails of his ship were in bad order, and his provisions nearly finished, he judged it best to give up further exploration.

Steering to the south-east, in bitter cold and stormy weather, he, too, sailed over the spot where Bouvet had marked land in his chart. Then heading for the Cape of Good Hope, he there repaired and provisioned his ship, and left once more for England, which he reached on 30th July 1775. The voyage had lasted more than three years, but during all that time he lost but four men, not one of them from scurvy, the dreaded disease which on all other ships had never failed to carry off so many victims.

Cook's Third and Last Voyage—His Death

Cook was now promoted to the rank of Post-Captain, and he was given an appointment which brought with it a good income. But he did not long stop at home to enjoy his honours. Before a year, had passed he had started on his third and last voyage of discovery.

But this time he was not to confine himself to the seas south of the equator.

Besides the question of the Great Unknown Land, there was another question which had filled men's minds for perhaps two hundred years before Cook's day, and over which people puzzled even down to the time when your grandfathers were young men. This was the question of what was called, the "North-West Passage."

To understand what is meant by the North-West Passage, you must know that it used to be the dream of sailors, and of many other men, to find a way round the north of America, whereby ships might sail to China and India without having to make the weary voyage round the Cape of Good Hope. For more than two hundred years men looked for this way, and at one time the English Government even offered a reward of £20,000 to the owners of any ship that should happen to find it. For more than two hundred years men searched, and lost their ships, and often their lives, in the search.

If you look at a map of North America, as it is now known, it may seem to you a simple thing to sail up Davis Strait past Greenland to Baffin's Bay, thence through Lancaster Sound, Barrow Strait, and Banks Strait, and so to Behring Strait and Asia: And that is what men thought, long ago. They had then no maps of that part of North America, but they believed that there must be such a passage round its northern end.

But the sea there is covered from year's end to year's end with ice, which opens, in parts, only now and again; and when it breaks up it is piled in wild confusion in what are called "hummocks." Any ship sailing into the open water between the moving masses of ice is very likely to be "nipped," and perhaps may never again get out. It was the terrible ice that prevented men from finding this North-West Passage. But always they believed that some day it would be found. Every explorer before Cook had tried it by way of Greenland and Davis Strait. Now it was thought that by starting from the other end, through Behring Strait (the narrow passage between Asia and America) there might be better fortune.

Cook offered to take command of this new expedition, and, on 12th July 1776, he sailed from Plymouth in his old ship, the *Resolution*. With him went a smaller vessel, the

Discovery, commanded by Captain Clerke, who as lieuten-ant, had been with Cook on his last voyage.

Cook's plans were to go by way of the Cape of Good Hope to Van Diemen's Land and New Zealand, thence to Otaheite, where he was to leave Omai, the man who had come from that island to England with Captain Furneaux, on the *Adventure*. From Otaheite he was to make for the coast of America, and so up to Behring Strait.

Whilst the *Resolution* lay in Table Bay, at the Cape of Good Hope, a terrible storm came on and blew for three days, doing great damage. The anchorage in Table Bay in those days gave little shelter to vessels during a gale from the north-west, and many a fine ship then dragged her anchors and went to pieces on the beach. Such storms often come up without much warning, and vessels were sometimes caught unprepared. Even when they were prepared, sometimes the wind blew with such violence that nothing could save them. On 5th November 1779 such a gale blew in Table Bay, and ship after ship dragged her anchor and was dashed to pieces. The English war-ship *Jupiter*, of 50 guns, was one of the few in the bay that rode the storm out in safety. But the *Sceptre*, of 64 guns, the Danish war-vessel *Oldenborg*, of 64 guns, and eight others, were all driven ashore and their crews drowned. Three waggon-loads of dead were taken next morning to be buried near the hospital, and about one hundred other bodies, terribly mangled, were buried in one grave on the beach. The *Sceptre* was taking home to England much of the plunder and many of the trophies taken at the battle of Seringapatam, in India, and these are now all lying under the sand of Table Bay.

It was in such a gale as this that the *Resolution* found herself, and she was the only vessel in the bay that did not drag her anchors. Cook was never caught unprepared. Luckily, perhaps, the *Discovery* had not then reached Table Bay. But she felt the full force of the storm out at sea, and lost one man overboard.

After leaving the Cape, rough weather followed the ships as they headed east past the storm-beaten Marion and Crozet Islands. Thence Cook went in search of Kerguelen Land, a large island discovered in 1772 by the French sailor Kerguelen. On this desolate spot Cook landed, and explored the whole island. Penguins and other sea-birds and seals were found in plenty, but no other form of life. Trees or shrubs there were none, but a small plant growing on the sides of the hills gave to them the look of being covered with green grass. In the bays enormous plants of seaweed were seen, some of them nearly 400 feet in length. Fastened to a rock by a bit of wire a bottle was found, in which, on a bit of parchment, was a record of the island having been visited in 1772 and 1773 by the French. Cook wrote on the back of the parchment that the *Resolution* and *Discovery* had also been there in 1776, and the bottle was then hidden in a cairn of stones. Perhaps, if you look, it may be there to this day.

The ships then left for Van Diemen's Land, where they

anchored on 26th January 1777. Here natives were seen, all entirely without clothing; they were quite friendly and harmless, and very easily alarmed by the sound of a gun. It is pitiful to think that this harmless race now no longer lives, and that the natives of Australia are also quickly dying out. Except in the far interior, it is seldom that an Australian "black-fellow" is now seen. Very soon there will be none left anywhere.

From Van Diemen's Land the ships now made for Queen Charlotte Sound, where they anchored on 12th February. This time, at first none of the Maori would venture on board; the sight of Omai, who had been with the *Adventure* when her boat's crew was murdered, seemed to alarm them. But after a little their alarm wore off, and they became again quite friendly. Even the chief who led the party that killed the boat's crew did not fear to come on board; and after so long a time, Captain Cook did not think it right to take any revenge on him. This was greatly to the regret of Omai, whose wishes always ran in the direction of killing his enemies whenever he had the chance.

Leaving New Zealand, the two ships now again headed for the Society Islands. On the way several islands were discovered, and many of those seen on the last voyage were revisited.

At every place there was the old story of thieving, and some of the cases now were so bad that Cook more than once took strong means to punish the natives, sometimes flogging them, sometimes destroying canoes, or burning houses. Once, at Anamooka, a thief was caught in the act of stealing, and he was given a dozen lashes and was ordered to pay a fine of a hog.

After this, no chiefs ever stole; they made their servants steal for them, and when the servants were punished the chiefs only laughed. It did not hurt *them!* Nor did the servants care much for a flogging: it did not keep them from stealing again. A better way of punishing was at last found. Every thief when caught had his head shaved by the ships' barbers; he was then a marked man, and was never again allowed to come on board either ship.

At Huaheine, Omai was put on shore, taking with him a huge quantity of presents. He had been very popular during his long stay in England, and probably he was very much spoiled by too much notice having been taken of him. Like most natives, Omai very quickly went back to the customs and dress, or want of dress, of his own people, and no good came from his visit to England. It is said that often afterwards in Huaheine he used to shoot with one of his Muskets at a man, just for the fun of seeing how far the musket could carry; and that with his pistols he often, for the pleasure of the thing, used to shoot persons of whom the king of the island wanted to get rid. Omai lived only about ten years after Cook left him, and no one was sorry when he died.

On 18th January 1778 high islands were sighted, part of a group till now unknown, a group which will live in history for all time, because of the terrible thing that happened there little more than a year later.

The islands now sighted were some of those named by Cook the Sandwich Islands. On two of them, Atooi and Oneeheow, Cook when he now landed was treated with extraordinary honour. Wherever he went, the natives threw themselves on the ground and covered their faces, till signs were made for them to rise. But in spite of this great respect, things were stolen from the ships, just as had been the case at other islands.

By the crews of the *Resolution* and *Discovery* these islands were looked on as a Paradise almost as lovely as Otaheite, and great was their sorrow when on 2nd February the ships sailed for the cold waters and snowy shores of North America. Mr. Gilbert, one of the officers of the *Discovery* says in his journal that they left the islands "with the greatest regret.... supposing all the pleasures of the voyage to be now at an end; having nothing to expect in future but excess of cold, hunger, and every kind of hardship and distress.

On 7th March the first American land was sighted. This was part of that coast which Sir Francis Drake two hundred years before had named New Albion, the part that is now known as Oregon. And here the "excess of cold," feared by Mr. Gilbert, began, for snow was lying on the hills. Owing to bad weather the two ships were more than three weeks in sailing about three hundred miles to the north, and it was not till 29th March that they anchored in a fine harbour, called Nootka Sound, in what is now known as Vancouver Island, part of the great Dominion of Canada.

Here indeed did the country differ from the lovely coral islands amongst which they had sailed so lately, islands to which officers and men longed to return. Here, instead of waving palm trees, were gloomy forests of pine; instead of beautiful hills covered to their tops with green trees and shrubs, were high mountains covered with snow. In place of the soft-skinned, smiling Tahitians, paddling in their canoes or swimming in the warm water round the ships, were natives who seemed both dirty and stupid. They had little to sell except skins and furs of bears and beavers, of sea-otters and other animals, articles not wanted by men whose wishes were all fixed on things they had left in sunny Otaheite.

At Nootka Sound the ships stayed four weeks, repairing the masts and rigging of the *Resolution*. Stormy weather followed them as they went north, and the *Resolution* sprang a bad leak, which gave the crew hard work at the pumps for some days. So stormy was the weather that it was not till the 2nd of May that the ships dared to run in towards the land. On every side were seen snow-clad mountains, Mount St. Elias, not far short of twenty thousand feet in height, towering over everything, a splendid sight in his glittering white coat. To the north of Mount St. Elias, in a corner of the great inlet which Cook named

Prince William's Sound, the ship's carpenters managed to stop the leak of the *Resolution.*

On this part of the coast the natives were very different from those of Nootka Sound. They were short and stout, and were clothed in the skins of seals and of other animals; only in their dirt were they something like the Nootka men. Their canoes too were different; they were made of the skins of seals stretched over a light wooden frame. In the centre of these canoes is a hole just big enough for a man to sit in with his legs pushed forward under the deck. Though so light that a man can easily lift one of the single canoes with one hand, they can safely go out in a very heavy sea, and the natives sail them with such skill that they can use their spears freely to kill seals, without any risk of upsetting.

The men that Cook saw here had a curious custom of slitting the upper lip till the gash looked like a second mouth, and in this they stuck shells, or bones, by way of ornament. Through the end of the nose also they stuck shells. They were very friendly, but, like most savages, terrible thieves.

The great bay called Cook's Inlet was next visited. Skirting along the coast from here, the ships were more than once in danger, for often the fog was so thick that they were only saved by letting go their anchors as soon as the sound of breakers was heard. Once, in thick fog, they ran between rocks so close to each other Cook says in his journal he would "not have ventured in a clear day," and they came, in the fog, "to such an anchoring place that I could not have chosen a better." He named a point of land near this spot Cape Providence.

Rounding the end of the Peninsula of Alaska, the ships felt their way, in cold, foggy weather, through shoals and reefs, up to Bristol Bay and Cape Newenham, round by the most westerly point of America, Cape Prince of Wales, and so through Behring Strait. In about latitude 65° the coast of Asia was sighted, and three boats' crews landed in St. Lawrence Bay, where friendly natives were met. These men used sledges drawn by dogs.

On 17th August what is called the "blink" of ice was seen to the north, and the same afternoon, in latitude 70° 44', the ships were stopped by large ice-fields. The land, near at hand on the American coast Cook named Icy Cape. Till 29th August he tried to find an opening through the ice. This way and that he pushed, but all to no purpose; it was not possible to get through; and Cook gave up the search for the passage round the north of America.

Whilst the ships were amongst the ice, as well as at many places along the coast, vast numbers of seals and walruses—sea-lions and sea-horses they were called— were seen on the rocks and on the floating ice; and many were killed and eaten by the crews. It is not very choice food, but the sailors thought it was better than salt junk.

Coming back along the American coast from Norton Sound to Cape Newenham, the ships found water so shallow that they were forced to keep farther out to sea. It was thought that the shoal water and the muddy look of the sea must be caused by some big river. And so it was. Had they but known it, that is where the mighty Yukon, one of the largest rivers in the world, flows into the sea—the great river on whose banks of late years so much gold has been found.

Cook now sailed again towards the south, meaning to revisit the Society Islands. Great was the delight of the sailors at the thought of getting back to the joys of their beloved coral islands. On 26th November the ships came in sight of Mowee, one of the Sandwich group, and soon afterwards they sighted Owhyhee—or, as it is now called, Hawaii. Neither of these islands had been seen on the first visit of the *Resolution* and *Discovery*. The sailors gazed with longing eyes at the beautiful shores, and at a vast mountain whose snow-clad top towered into the sky to a height of near fourteen thousand feet.

But though canoes brought out food and fruit, the ships did not anchor till they had worked their way round the south end of the island into Karakakooa Bay. Here hundreds of canoes, crowded with natives, came off; the beach was covered with people, and hundreds more, like shoals of fish, swam around the ships. Nowhere in his travels had Cook seen such crowds.

And now a strange thing was noticed! Wherever Captain Cook went, he was treated by the people as if he were something more than man. Priests put over his shoulders a red cloth, which to them was sacred, used only to drape their idols. They fell on their faces before him; they came to him with offerings of pigs and of fowls, priests solemnly chanting the while. In everything they treated him as if they believed him to be a God.

Very long ago there had lived in this island a great chief named Orono. After Orono's wife died, he left the island, and sailed away to foreign lands. But before sailing, he told his people that long years afterwards he would come back "on an island bearing cocoa-nut trees, swine, and dogs."

Long the people had looked for Orono, and now, at last, he had come! Who could the strangers be who came to their shores in ships as big as islands, in ships that had treelike things growing out of them? Who could they be but Orono and his friends? And so the people worshipped Cook, and thought that he and all his sailors were more than mortal.

But after a few weeks things began to change. One of the *Resolution's* men died, and was buried on shore. It may have been that the natives thought it strange that one of Orono's friends should die. Perhaps, too, they grew tired of supplying the ships with so many pigs and so many cocoa-nuts. Then some of the sailors gave offence by taking the images from a native temple; and soon the people began to wish that Orono would go away.

On 4th February 1779, to the relief of the natives, the ships sailed. Unluckily, it chanced that in a violent gale a few days later the *Resolution* badly damaged her foremast, and in less than a week the two vessels were back in Karakakooa Bay.

Now all was changed. The chiefs were no longer friendly; there was quarrel after quarrel, and the natives stole everything they could lay hands on. Once or twice men on shore were attacked with stones, and at last one of the *Discovery's* boats was stolen from her moorings.

Cook was very angry, and on 14th February he went himself on shore with an armed boat's crew and nine marines to try to get it back. Failing that, he meant to bring the king on board, and to keep him there till the stolen boat was given up.

There was a good deal of excitement on shore, and the natives crowded round. Cook had not been able to persuade the king to come with him, and he did not want to use force. He was walking down the beach back to his boat, when suddenly a native from another part of the bay ran hurriedly into the crowd shouting, "It is war. They have killed a chief." At once all was confusion. The natives rushed to seize the muskets of the marines, and a stone was thrown at Cook, who fired with small shot at the man who threw it, but without doing much damage. The native was then about to throw his spear, when Cook knocked him down with the butt of his double-barreled gun. Then he was forced to fire at a man who was in the act of throwing a spear. Showers of stones were hurled at the marines, and they, without waiting for orders, began to fire. Captain Cook waved his hand and shouted to them to stop firing, but in the noise and confusion his orders were not heard.

The natives now made a rush, and four of the marines were killed; the others managed to get into one of the boats which had come in close to the shore.

Cook was left alone on the beach. He turned to walk towards the boat, when a chief ran up and struck him with a heavy club on the back of the head. The captain staggered forward and fell on his hands and knees, dropping his gun. As he struggled to his feet, another native, rushing in, stabbed him in the back of the neck, and he fell in the water. Then the natives poured over him, trying to keep him under. Again and again he got his head above water, fighting for his life. Again and again the weight of numbers forced him back. And now, at length, strength left him; there was none to help; he could struggle no longer. He was stabbed by every native who could get near enough to him; his head was battered against a rock till he ceased to move.

So sank and died Captain James Cook, the greatest navigator of all time, a man whom all the world honours, whose name will live as long as the English language is spoken.

His bones were recovered some days later, but only his bones, and not all of them. It is likely that the rest of him was burned, for the natives of Owhyhee were not cannibals.

They were sad ships that left Karakakooa Bay a week

later; sad were his sailors that their officers allowed them to take no fitting revenge. And a sad day it was for England when the news came home of the death of her great sailor in the far Pacific.